AF577370

Our opponent comes to town wearing a cocky grin,
but they don't know we're hungry for a win!

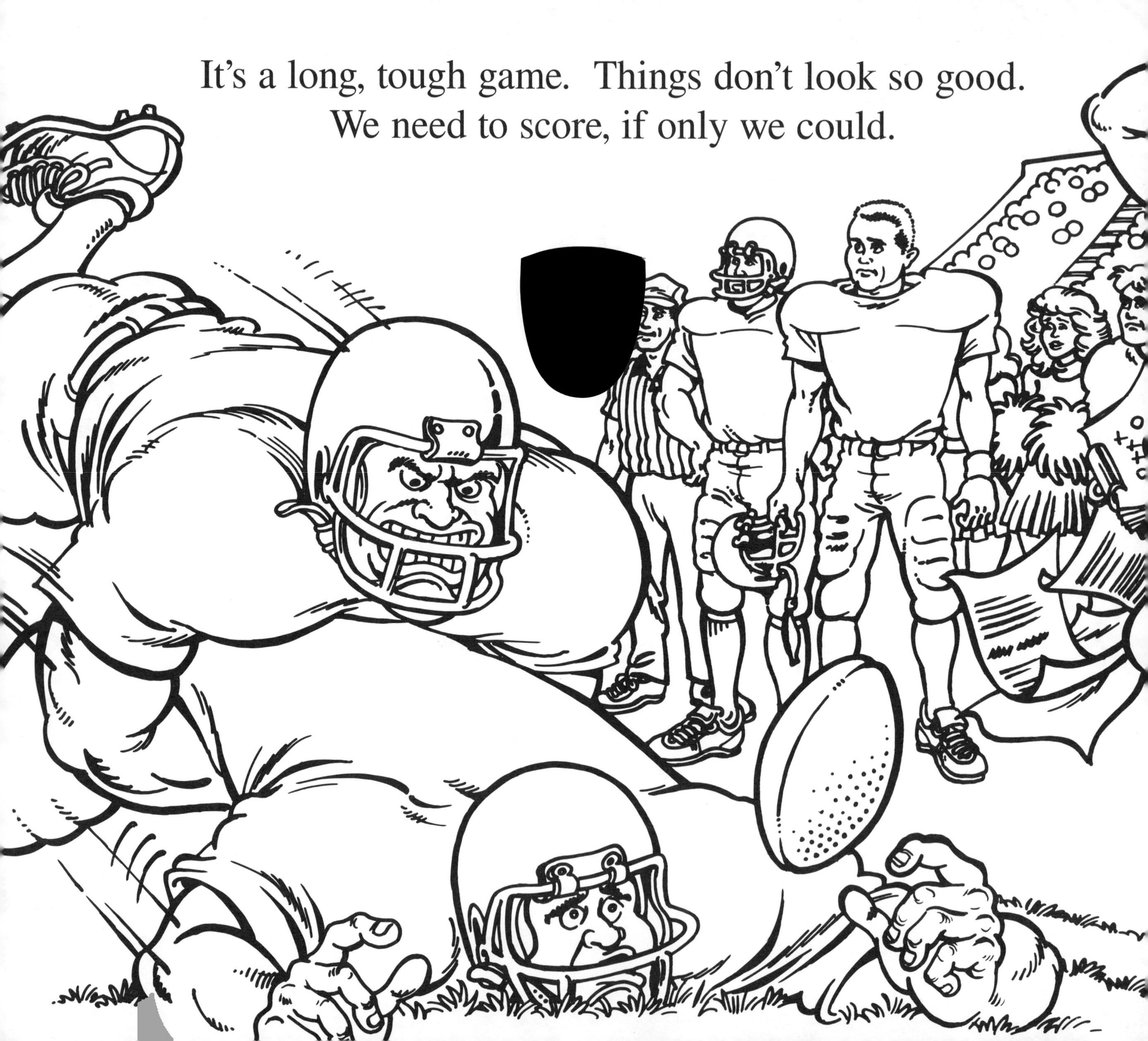
It's a long, tough game. Things don't look so good.
We need to score, if only we could.

Some of the guys could use a rest,
but we're going to win 'cause my team's the best!

Our opponent uses another twist...
Look out guys,
it’s a quarterback blitz!

The quarterback’s down, they call me in.
Coach looks at me and says with a grin,

“This is your chance kid--you know our plays by heart.
You’ve got talent, and I know you’re smart.”

"Get in there now.
Show me what you can do.
The team really
needs a score.
It's all up to you!"

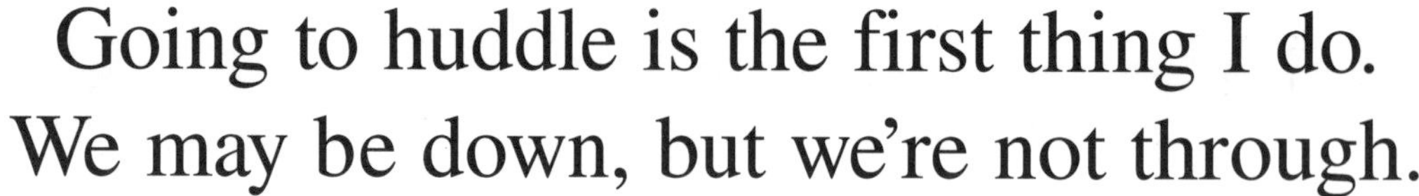

Going to huddle is the first thing I do.
We may be down, but we're not through.

TIME 0:34
ME 17 VISITOR 20

There's not much time to make a score...
Just three more plays to close the door.

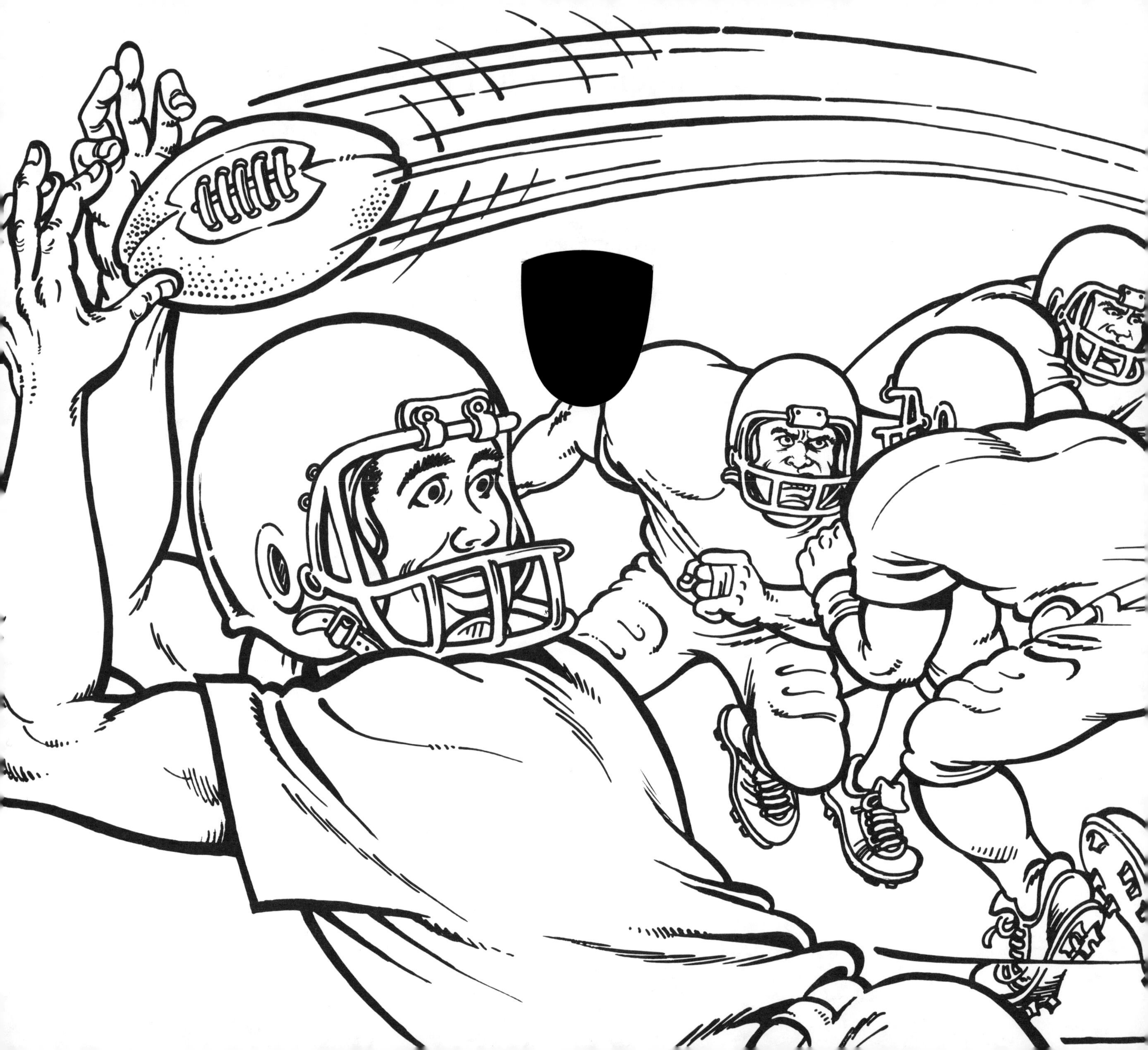

The center snaps the ball. I drop back to pass.
It goes to the wide receiver 'cause he's so fast.

I hand off to the fullback. He takes it to the 10.
We're going to get up and do it again!

I fake a pass and bootleg a run,
then score the winning touchdown at the sound of the gun!

The fans all cheer as I receive the game ball.
Once again, my team stands tall.

TV4

We've won the game and everyone around
wants to know how it feels to score the winning touchdown.

All I can say is “I love the game,
and doing my best is always my aim.”

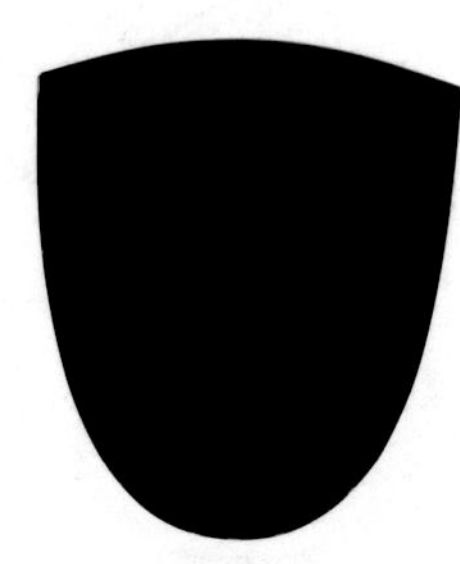

U.S. Pat. No. 5,238,345
PATENT PENDING

Copyright © 1996 Picture Me Books, Inc., Akron, Ohio. All rights reserved.
No part of this publication may be reproduced, stored in a retrieval system or transmitted in any form by any means, electronic, mechanical, photocopying, recording or otherwise without prior permission of the publisher.

Copyright © 1996 NFL Properties, Inc.
Published under license by Picture Me Books, Inc,. Akron, Ohio.

The name "Picture Me Books" and the device PICTURE Me BOOKS ® are Registered Trade Marks of Picture Me Books, Inc.

Picture Me Books, Inc., is also the owner of the mark PICTURE Me BOOKS ™

The names, symbols, emblems, designs, logos, and other indicia of the National Football League and its member clubs are registered in the U.S. Patent and Trademark Office and are protectable against unauthorized use.

Manufactured in the U.S.A.

For premium and promotional sales, please call (800) 762-6775.